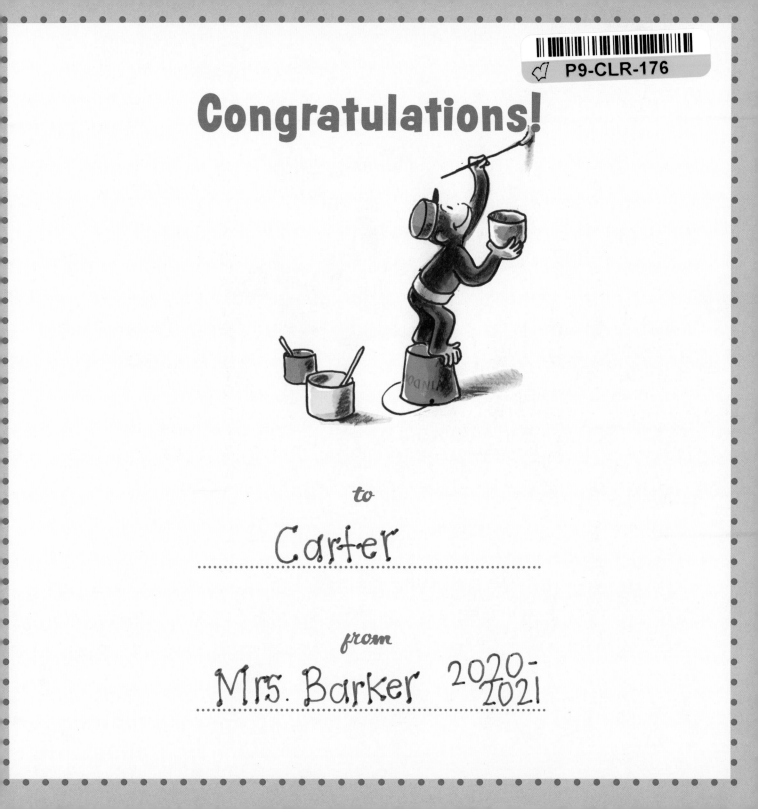

Congratulations!

to

Carter

from

Mrs. Barker 2020-2021

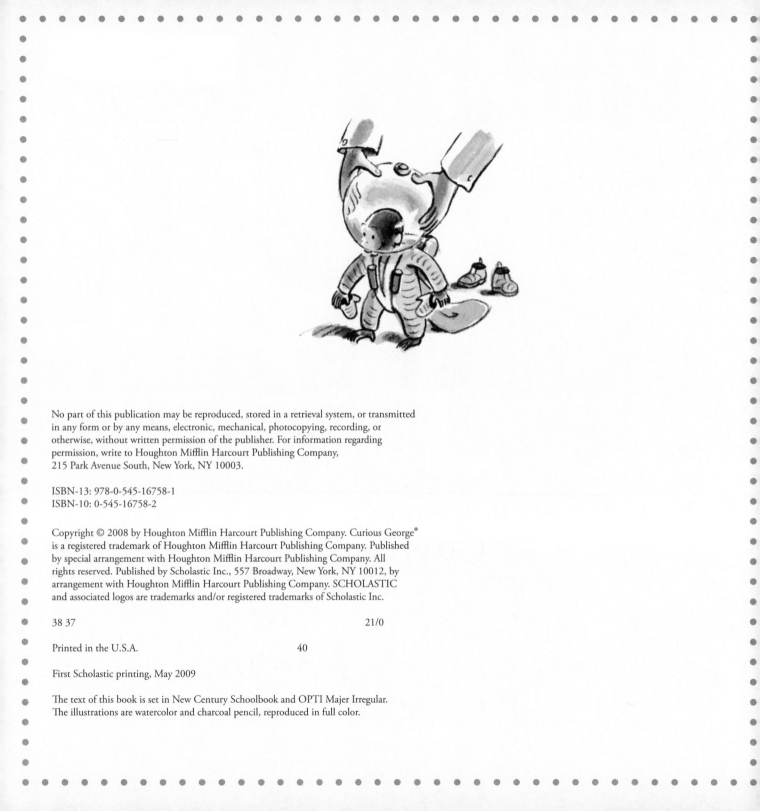

ISBN-13: 978-0-545-16758-1
ISBN-10: 0-545-16758-2

38 37   21/0

Printed in the U.S.A.   40

First Scholastic printing, May 2009

The text of this book is set in New Century Schoolbook and OPTI Majer Irregular.
The illustrations are watercolor and charcoal pencil, reproduced in full color.

Curious You
On Your Way!

Written by Kathleen W. Zoehfeld   Illustrated by H. A. Rey

SCHOLASTIC INC.
New York Toronto London Auckland Sydney
Mexico City New Delhi Hong Kong Buenos Aires

HIP, HIP, HOORAY!

You've done great things.

The whole world is proud of **YOU** today.

You've learned so much.
You studied hard.

And put your brains to the test.

You played on the team!

Of course, the time comes when
a curious monkey needs to **break free!**

Even if it means you don't know exactly
where you're going . . .

or what
will come next.

So much to **see!**

So much to **try!**

What should you **do?**

It's
up
to
YOU.

Just **follow your dreams** and you'll soar.

You may feel
a little frightened
at times. But . . .
hold on tight!

You'll **see sights** that take your breath away!

You'll find the spot where you most want to land.

Oh, what a place it will be!

The thrill of discovery will be yours.

And if things don't work out quite as you had planned... **don't worry!**

All great explorers **bump** and **crash** sometimes.

There
will
always
be
new
heights
to
reach.

Whatever you do,
you will
find your own style.

Even if it **surprises** a few!

You'll **give to others** in ways that only **you** can.

And you will
make **new friends.**

The world needs
you **now.**

You've got

BIG

ideas.

The feats you imagine
you'll just **HAVE** to try . . .
and imagination can lead to invention.

Before you know it,

the **SPOTLIGHT** will be on **YOU**.

What will your story be?
Bold and inspiring—
a tale of curiosity
and brave exploration!

Everyone will line up to see!

And if the path that you choose gets rocky and rough—

whenever you feel all alone—

remember,

we're with you all the way.
Today, tomorrow . . .

. . . and every day!

We're proud of **curious YOU.**